Little Wombat

Story by Chris Mansell   Illustrations by Cheryl Westenberg

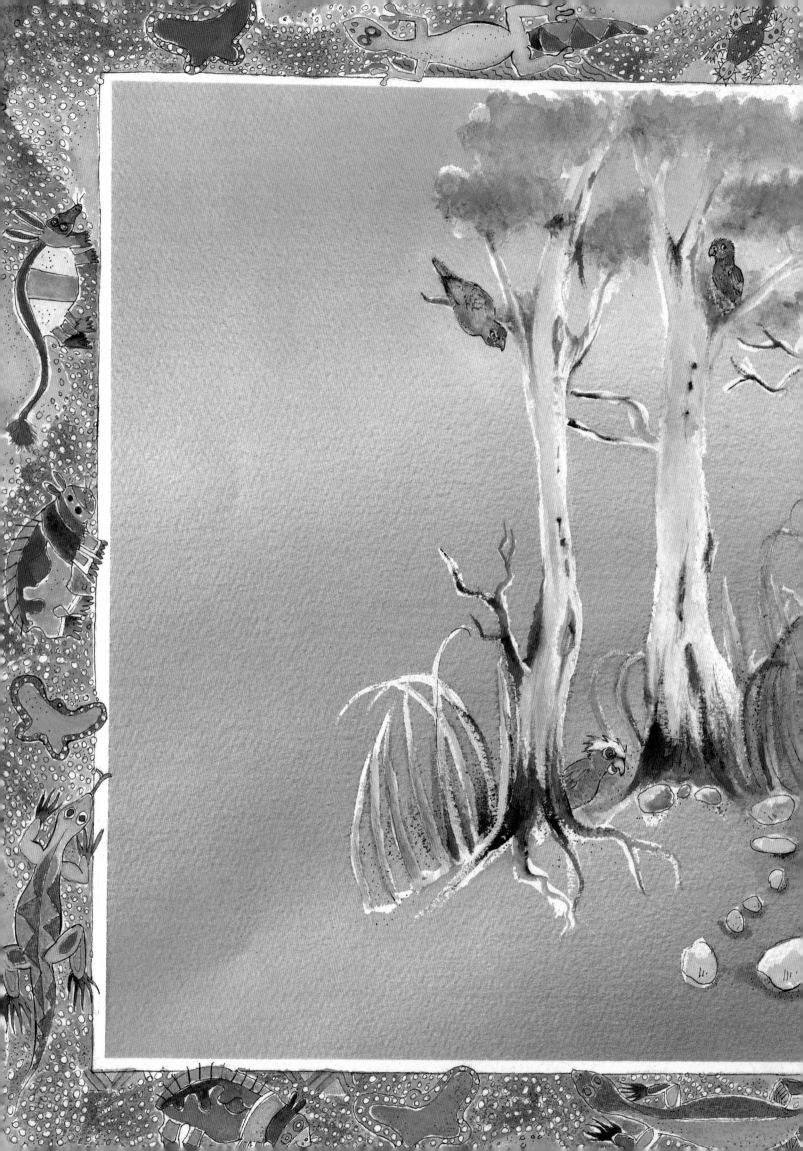

On a sunny afternoon, suitable for wombat snoozing, the little wombat stretched on her back in the sun and talked with her Aunty Plump Cushion.

"People have trouble filling up one name", the little wombat said to Aunty Plump Cushion, "but I could fill several, I'm sure".

Aunty Plump Cushion rolled over and squinted in the sun and passed little wombat some grass-root juice. She remembered when she had had to choose her own name as all little wombats must.

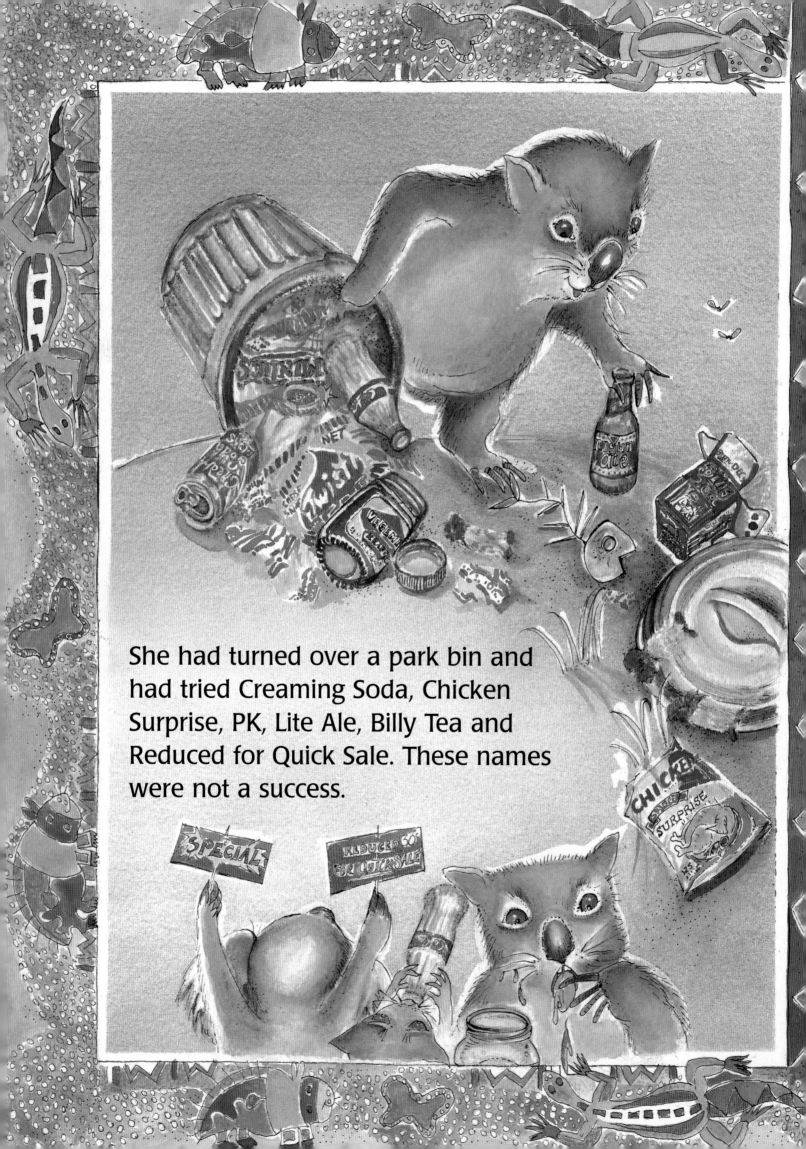

She had turned over a park bin and had tried Creaming Soda, Chicken Surprise, PK, Lite Ale, Billy Tea and Reduced for Quick Sale. These names were not a success.

Plump Cushion was more her style
and she had been glad of the advice
of Granny Gumboot.

Little wombat wanted a real name
that showed who she was.

But she really didn't know what...

...although she'd always fancied
herself as a bit of a tightrope walker.

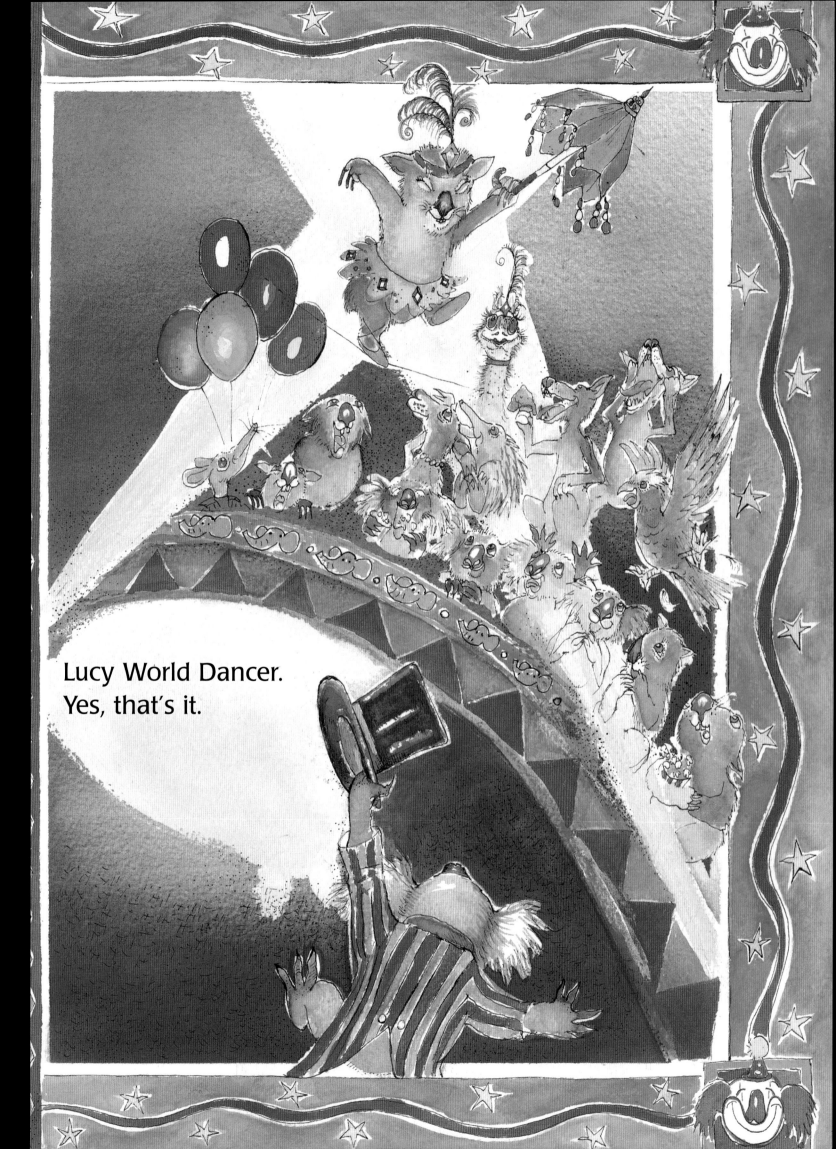

Lucy World Dancer.
Yes, that's it.

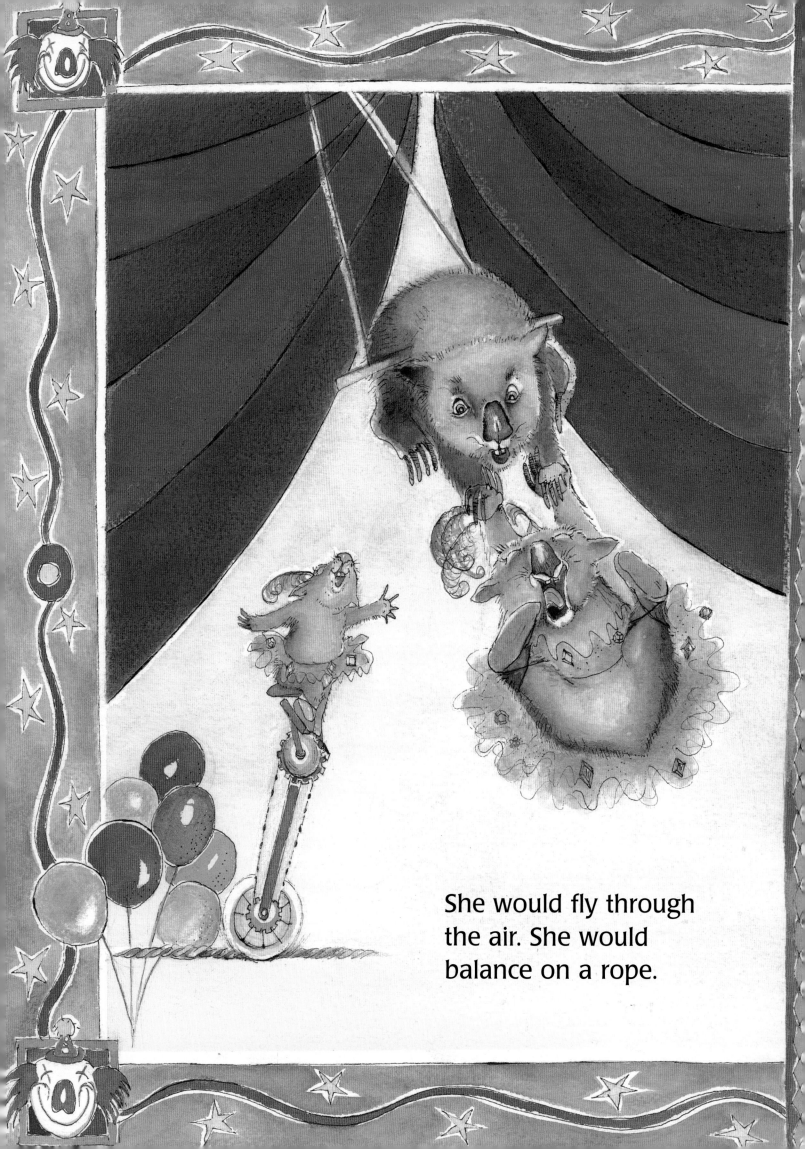

She would fly through the air. She would balance on a rope.

She would sing in the sky.
She would be top of the
big top.

"Or", she said to Aunty, "Kip Thistlethrower, a clown in a big yellow costume with a little blue umbrella. And I could do tumbling tricks and...".

Aunty Plump Cushion looked at the little wombat. Little wombat looked at her short legs. Little wombat thought again.

"What about", she said to Aunty Plump Cushion, "What about Patricia Fancyknit? I could sew, I could make things.

I could...". She looked at her clumsy claws.

"Or Iodine Cleansheet! A nurse!" But
the sad fact that she loved digging in
the dirt made her think again.

"Dirt! I'll be an archaeologist!
Dinny Digsworth then."

"I'm strong—Jawcutter Pullen? A dentist?" she asked Aunty with less and less hope.

Aunty pursed her lips and shook her head.

"No", said little wombat, "I'll be Whizzpast Roaring Gleam, famous motorcycle racer! I'll be the first wombat to win the Australian Grand Prix. I'll be fast! I'll be famous! I'll be...".

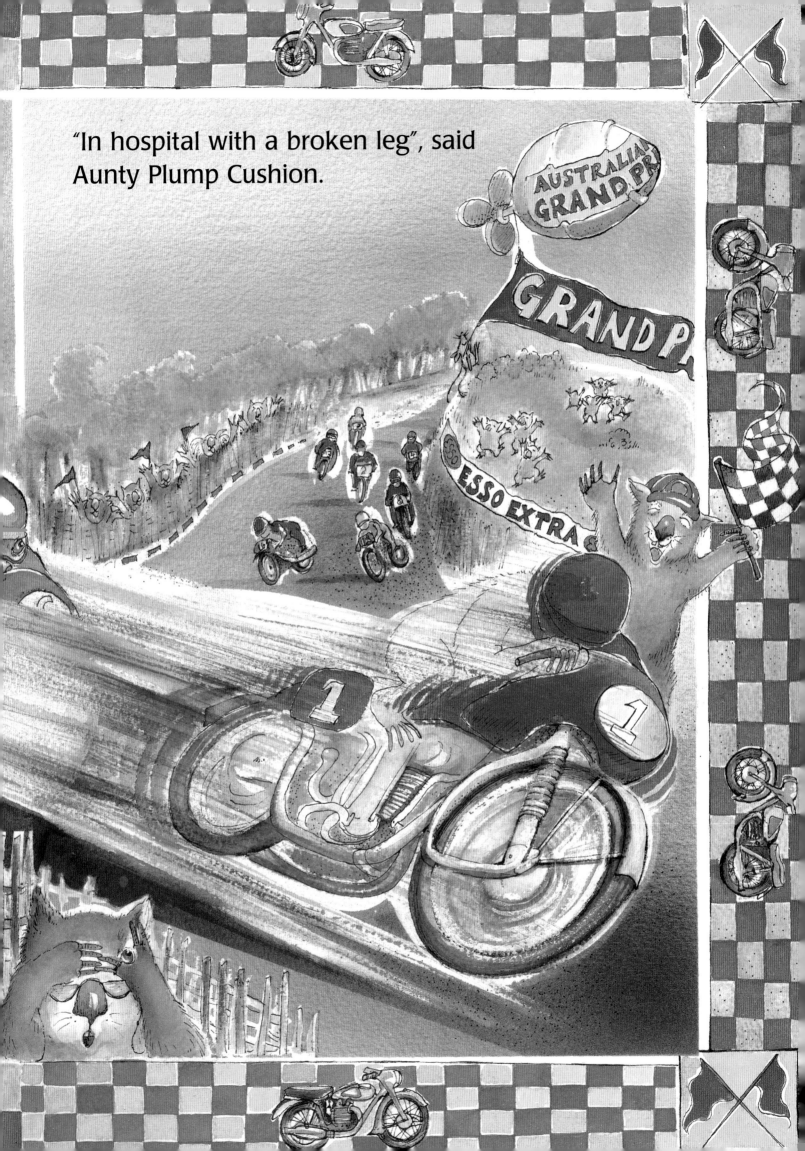

"In hospital with a broken leg", said Aunty Plump Cushion.

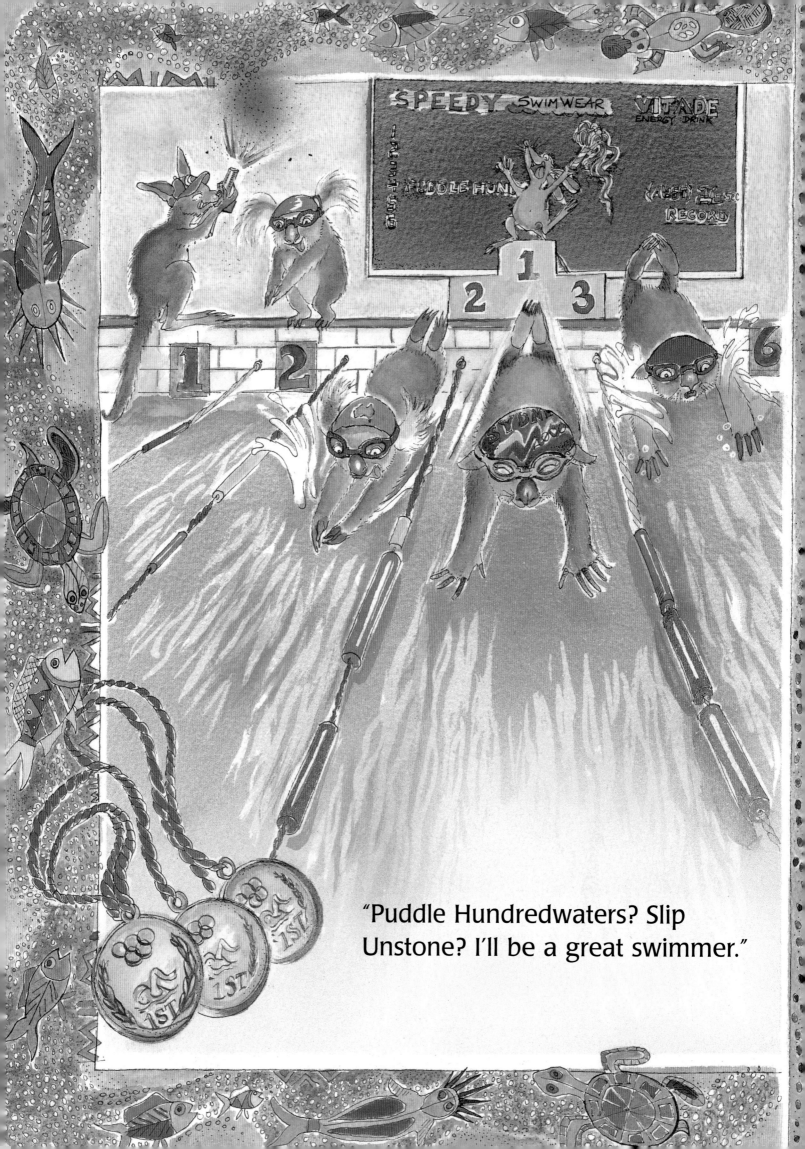

"Puddle Hundredwaters? Slip Unstone? I'll be a great swimmer."

Aunty raised her eyebrows and little
wombat wondered if she was going
to end up with a name like Granny
Gumboot or Papa Toadhead. Oh dear.
"Think of something... less energetic"
said Aunty Plump Cushion.

But there were only boring things left. Things you had to sit down for.

Although she did think that Geranium Lake might be a nice name for an artist,

and suggested Pyjama
Pencilwort (a writer), but Aunty
knew writers and artists came to bad ends.

The little wombat thought that there were no names left in the world. She curled one strong paw over the other and arched her back in the sun and was as warm as a stone.

"Aunty", she said just as she was about to fall asleep, "I think I've found my name".

"Oh yes", said Aunty, expecting
something very very silly.
"I'm going to be Boulder Einstein-Wombat,
because I want to be smart as stone."

Aunty sighed, she never
had any luck helping
with names. Smart
as stone! The little
wombat has got
rocks in her head!
She's as mad as
an emu!

"I'll sit in the sun", said Boulder, "and listen to the bush sing like music and be warm and brown and wombat-shaped.
That's what I'll be".

"My dear Boulder", Aunty Plump
Cushion finally smiled, "I'm glad
you chose well—

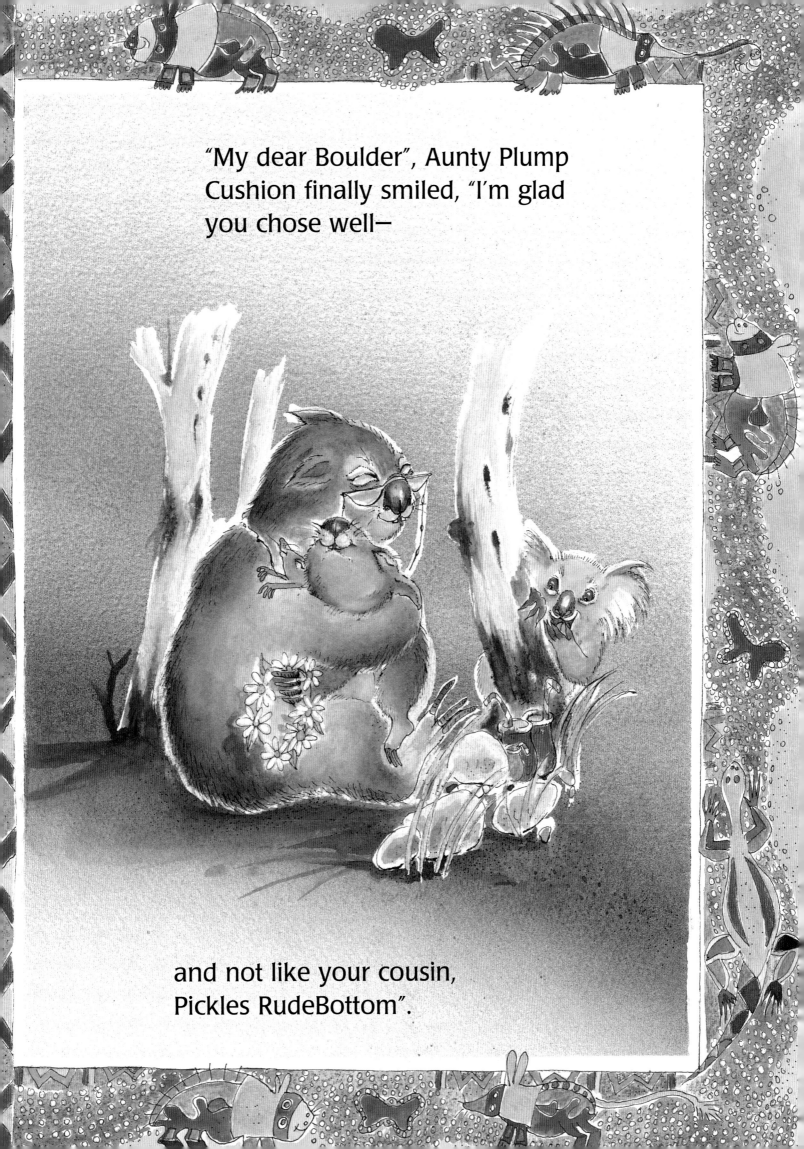

and not like your cousin,
Pickles RudeBottom".

First published by New Holland Publishers (Australia),
an imprint of National Book Distributors Pty Ltd
3/2 Aquatic Drive, Frenchs Forest, NSW 2086, Australia

Story © Chris Mansell
Illustrations © Cheryl Westenberg
Published Edition © New Holland Publishers (Australia), 1995

Printed in Hong Kong by Everbest Printing Co. Ltd

ISBN 1 86436 082 8